Alain St. Michelle

DATE DUE

SEP 2 0 [illegible]

My p[...]
Don't [...]
Don't [...]
Don't [...]
And in survey questions:
Did you do your homework?
Did you study?
Did you get to school on time?
And in minisermons:
Be a role model for your little brother.
Be a credit to your parents.
Be a good citizen, above all.
America may be freer than my native Haiti,
But try telling that to my parents,
Who still treat me like a little bébé.
And still practice authoritarian rule
In their own personal government-in-exile.

————————————

★ "Glenn delivers a starkly realistic view of modern high school life."
—*School Library Journal*, starred review

DISCARDED

OTHER PUFFIN BOOKS YOU MAY ENJOY

Who Killed Mr. Chippendale?

A Mystery in Poems

MEL GLENN

PUFFIN BOOKS

PUFFIN BOOKS

Published by the Penguin Group

Penguin Putnam Books for Young Readers,

345 Hudson Street, New York, New York 10014, U.S.A.

Penguin Books Ltd, 27 Wrights Lane, London W8 5TZ, England

Penguin Books Australia Ltd, Ringwood, Victoria, Australia

Penguin Books Canada Ltd, 10 Alcorn Avenue, Toronto, Ontario, Canada M4V 3B2

Penguin Books (N.Z.) Ltd, 182-190 Wairau Road, Auckland 10, New Zealand

Penguin Books Ltd, Registered Offices: Harmondsworth, Middlesex, England

First published in the United States of America by Lodestar Books,
an affiliate of Dutton Children's Books, a division of Penguin Books USA Inc., 1996
Published by Puffin Books,
a member of Penguin Putnam Books for Young Readers, 1999

5 7 9 10 8 6 4

Copyright © Mel Glenn, 1996
All rights reserved

THE LIBRARY OF CONGRESS HAS CATALOGED THE LODESTAR EDITION AS FOLLOWS:
Glenn, Mel.
Who killed Mr. Chippendale?: a mystery in poems / Mel Glenn.
p. cm.
"Lodestar books."
Summary: Free verse poems describe the reactions of students, colleagues, and
others when a high school teacher is shot to death as the school day begins.
ISBN 0-525-67530-2 (alk. paper)
[1. High schools—Fiction. 2. Teacher-student relationships—Fiction.
3. Death—Fiction. 4. Schools—Fiction. 5. Mystery and detective stories.]
I. Title. PZ7.G845Wh 1996 [Fic]—dc20 95-52600 CIP AC

Puffin Books ISBN 0-14-038513-4

Printed in the United States of America

Except in the United States of America, this book is sold subject to the condition that
it shall not, by way of trade or otherwise, be lent, re-sold, hired out, or otherwise
circulated without the publisher's prior consent in any form of binding or cover
other than that in which it is published and without a similar condition
including this condition being imposed on the subsequent purchaser.

FOR JONATHAN,
MY SON,
WHO HAS ALL THE
WRITE STUFF

ROBERT CHIPPENDALE

In the early morning light,
Robert Chippendale, English teacher
For more than twenty years at Tower High,
Punches in at 7:04.
He will never touch the card again.
He is unaware that before this day, February 27, is
    over,
Tower will be rocked by murder,
Spotlighted by the ten o'clock news and
Denounced by the general public.
Dressed in a blue jogging suit,
He carries over his shoulder his old sports jacket
And newer slacks—his school clothes—in a garment
    bag,
Which he hangs in the teachers' locker room.
Lightly jogging down the stairs to the back door,
He pushes it open
To cross the short path to the running track.
He lets his mind wander while he stretches,
Pretending he is somewhere else:
The sand dunes of the Cape, the boardwalk by the
    beach.
He glances back at the school,
A looming gray citadel
With rounded arches and bulky minarets.
In a few minutes, the morning quiet will be shattered

By the babble of two thousand students—
Not a melting pot, but a multicultural mix,
Slouching its way toward Tower
With the customary cynicism of youth.
But now the school stands tall and quiet
Amid the working-class world
Of fast food places and auto repair shops.
He thinks he hears his name being called from beyond
    the fence.
"Hey, Mr. Chippendale," a girl's voice floats by,
But the sound and shape of the girl
Are gone before he can recognize either.
He hates his name; it has always caused him pain—
The written equivalent of Cyrano's nose,
The title of a cabinet maker, two squirrels,
A club for male strippers, or, worst of all,
The sound-alike name of a romanticized Latin teacher,
    Mr. Chips.
Is it too late to change his name, his life?
Seasons spent running in circles,
Starting and stopping at the same point on the track,
A metaphor, he thinks, for his teaching career,
Now rutted like the track itself,
In the soft years of familiarity.
He bends down to retie his laces
And notices that the air is surprisingly mild.
He does not see the face inside the red-hooded
    sweatshirt,

The body that bowls him over.
Lying sprawled on the ground
Chippendale tries to find the face,
The morning sun blocking his view.
He certainly hears the torrent of words:

Hey, man, watch where you goin'.

Ain'tcha heard of excuse me?

Hey, I'm talkin' to you.

Chippendale thinks, a morning run cancelled,

An incident report to the dean,

A trip to the principal's office.

Not worth it, no way, not on this glorious winter's day.

The voice again:

Hey, man, where you goin'?

You owe me an apology.

You think I'm nobody?

Something psychotically edgy in the voice,

More of a reason to let it drop.

As Chippendale gets up,

He watches the red-hooded sweatshirt pick up a long,
   thin package

And head through the back door, into the school,

Saying over his shoulder,

Listen to me,

Who do you think you are,

A movie star or somethin'?

ROBERT CHIPPENDALE

A good question, he thinks, while s-t-r-e-t-c-h-i-n-g.
Who am I?
Average height and average weight, no close relations.
Average person waiting on the movie line, single.
Description: light, curly brown hair; pleasant face;
    brown eyes.
Nothing special about him, the staff would say,
A little bit formal, reserved, if you will,
Even after twenty years at Tower.
A little bit nuts about running, but
Not outside the parameters of normalcy,
Even for teachers.
Is he happy?
Who could know?
Who wonders what teachers think behind their lesson
    plans?
He begins to run around the quarter-mile oval,
Checks his watch and looks at the sky, which
Threads out its ribbons of light.
Nearing the end of his second lap,
He thinks he hears several popping sounds,
Looks around, sees nothing.
He is ten yards into his third lap when the shot rings
    out.
He does not see, hear, or feel the bullet
That explodes his brain like a star-burst rocket.
He is dead before he hits the ground,
Instant blackness covering all.

KARYN MILLER

Looking at her nails—sleek perfection—
Admiring her professional skill,
Then glancing out the window
To escape a math-induced stupor, she saw
The familiar figure of Mr. C. (as most called him)
Run a few measured steps.
A sliver of memory, a 65 the term before,
A fair grade considering she did not like
English all that much, nothing personal, mind you.
She couldn't wait for the bell to ring
To end the period—to end high school,
So she could launch herself into the real world,
Prove to her mother
She could bring home a good salary instead of poor
    grades.
While her teacher attacked a theorem with droning
    insistence,
She stared at the running form an instant longer,
Heard a crackling sound and watched
His head lift off his shoulders
And fly out in various directions.
A scream choked in her throat,
Escaping finally in a shrill cry,
"He's shot! He's shot!
Help me! Help me!"

MIKE CURRY

Who's shot?
What happened? Where?
See anythin'?
> *Please stay in your rooms.*

Gotta get into the hall.
Whaddya hear?
Four people shot?
Cool!
Maybe the principal got it too.
> *Please stay in your rooms.*

Teacher's keepin' us in.
Whaddya mean, where was I? Bathroom, man.
You can't make us sit down.
I'm outta here, man.
Whoa, where'd all the cops come from?
> *Please stay in your rooms.*

Chippendale?
You're kiddin' me, man,
Had him two terms ago,
Bor-ing, no life to him.
Then and now, ha, ha.
> *Please stay in your rooms.*

Yeah, right.
Hey, maybe I'll make the ten o'clock news.
Cool!

RUSSELL FRANKS, PRINCIPAL

I'm afraid you reporters will have to leave now.
Please exit through the front door,
Or I'll have to get a security guard to escort you out.
Yes, I have a brief statement to make:

At approximately 7:30 this morning,
The body of one of our teachers
Was found on the school's track.
We are withholding disclosure of his name
Pending notification of next of kin.
The cause of death is yet to be determined,
But we believe it may have been a massive coronary.
Reports and rumors of any other cause of death
Are speculative and unfounded.
I will not comment further,
Except to say that the teacher in question
Enjoyed the respect of his peers and
The admiration of his students.
He will be sorely missed.
That is all I can say for now.

Questions? No, I won't take any questions.
I have no answers, either.

JACK HASKELL, REPORTER

Yeah, I'm a real reporter,
See my press badge?
Yeah, it's gonna be in the paper,
If you give me somethin' I can use.
Help me out, son.
I heard it on the scanner,
Raced over here only to find
The principal's stonewallin' and
The cops are screwin' around
And I'm comin' up on deadline.
So whaddya say, you got somethin' for me?
We heard he was shot—Is that true?
Someone had it in for him—Is that true?
He was a tough teacher—Is that true?
Was he foolin' around with any of his students,
Male or female?
What?
He didn't allow students to talk in class.
He didn't allow students to chew gum.
He didn't allow students to go to the bathroom.
Can I quote you on that?
What's your name? Mike?
Mike, you're not pullin' my leg now, are you, son?
Though I've seen people shot for less.

Oh my God,
It's true, then,
Mr. C., oh my God,
I can't believe it.
I hope no one sees me crying.
I hope his soul goes straight to heaven.
What that man did for me,
I don't have the words for it.
He made me feel smarter than I am.
He praised my poetry.
He thought I was college material.
You know, in many ways he reminded me of my
    father:
Quiet,
Modest,
Brave.
When's the funeral?
I must go and pay my respects.
He was the best teacher I ever had.
You can ask my twin.

DELIA CAMPBELL

Oh my God,
It's true, then,
Mr. C., oh my God,
I can't believe it.
I hope no one sees me laughing.
I hope his soul goes straight to hell.
What that man did to me,
I don't have the words for it.
He made me feel stupider than I am.
He trashed my poetry.
He thought I wasn't college material.
You know, in many ways he reminded me of my
    father:
Loud,
Vain,
Cowardly.
When's the funeral?
You won't catch me anywhere near it.
He was the worst teacher I ever had.
You can ask my twin.

EUGENE BRAYMORE, POLICE CAPTAIN

PRESS MEMO

Robert Chippendale, a teacher
at Tower High, was killed by
a single bullet fired from
the roof of the building
yesterday. We're investigating
the possibility of other shots
fired. At present we have no
suspect, no weapon, no rationale for this despicable act.
We have cordoned off the area
and are proceeding with our
investigation.

POSSIBLE MOTIVES

"He dissed me."

"I needed the money."

"He looked at me funny."

"I caught him with my ..."

"He stole from me."

"I heard voices."

"I tell you it was an accident."

"I swear it wasn't personal."

"For kicks, man."

PERSONAL MEMO

In the lineup of possible reasons,
Not a single one has stepped forward
To claim responsibility.

REMINDER

Check out deceased's political affiliations.

CAROL DEE DELANEY

CD—get it?
That's what my friends call me.
Must be a sign, right?
Music's the only thing that matters, man.
Can't tell you how many CDs I have
Or how many concerts I've been to.
I only know that the best part of my life
Is when I'm screamin' my brains out,
Forgetting for an hour or so,
The things people want me to do.
It's so intense, man.
Last week when my favorite rock singer died,
I shut myself in my room,
Cried for two days,
And played all his songs.
Who died also?
Wasn't he a teacher at our school or somethin'?
No, I'm not goin' to the funeral.
He ain't nobody important, is he?
What CDs did he cut?

ANGELA FALCONE, GUIDANCE COUNSELOR

His death doesn't match his life, I think,
As I walk up the front steps of the church.
It doesn't fit; it doesn't make sense, dammit.
Who did it and why?
Oh, Robert, we should have been closer.
We are all islands,
Loosely chained by the bonds of love.
But such ties erode and
Islands become even more isolated,
Without connections to link them.
Oh, Robert, we should have been closer.
For others I had time,
Medic in the teenage wars,
Treating casualties of homes
Damaged by dysfunction,
Crippled by confrontation.
Oh, Robert, we should have been closer.
We were,
Once, you know.

FATHER FRANCIS BOSCO
ANGELA FALCONE, GUIDANCE COUNSELOR

I am truly sorry at his passing. . . .

> *What passing? His head was blown off.*

His principal, Mr. Franks, is here. . . .

> *The worm, he'd rather be anyplace else.*

Mr. Chippendale was a loyal and industrious
worker. . . .

> *Makes him sound like an ant.*

He was a teacher, a prized member of the
community. . . .

> *It takes his death to find that out?*

It is a difficult task to be a teacher these days. . . .

> *More than you realize, Father.*

Who else but a teacher can mold the future? . . .

> *Bend steel with his bare hands?*

Who else can spend the day with future authors? . . .

> *And criminals.*

Who else can pass on our rich culture? . . .

> *MTV?*

So let us not forget him. . . .

> *They already have his replacement.*

A man who will teach for eternity in heaven. . . .

> *What, no prep periods?*

Let us pray.

> *Forgive me Father.*
> *There is so much you didn't say,*
> *So much you don't know.*

My mother would kill me if
She ever found out I stepped into a church,
Even for this.
Me, who went to Hebrew school,
Me, who was bat mitzvahed,
Me, who fasted last Yom Kippur for the first time.
I don't know any of the prayers here.
I don't know if I should kneel.
I don't know how to express the pain I feel.
I only know Mr. Chippendale's dead
And that I had to come here to say good-bye.
He'd always kid me,
Gently, of course,
About asking so many questions.
He'd always answer them.
My mother would kill me if
She ever found out I stepped into a church.
She'd cry for my lost soul.
In the meantime, I'll cry for his.
Forgive me, but I have one more question:
Why did he have to die?

GARY LOCKHART, NEIGHBORHOOD RESIDENT

What's happenin' over by the church?
That's the funeral for Mr. What'shisname,
You know, the teacher who got shot at the school.
Well, what can you expect from a bunch of hoodlums?
They all lie, steal, do drugs, all of 'em.
Animals, you know what I mean.
Yeah, my son went to Tower,
About a year 'fore he dropped out.
He was a wild one, my son,
Just like me when I was his age.
Sure, I told him to stay in school,
Told him he'd be nothin' but a bum,
That he'd wind up in jail,
Or end up dead.
Didn't do no good, though.
He started hangin' out with a bad crowd,
Animals, you know what I mean.
I ain't seen him in years now.
He never comes 'round no more.
You'd think I drove him away or somethin'.
You'd think I didn't teach him nothin'.

FROM: BOARD OF EDUCATION
TO: ROBERT CHIPPENDALE
RE: HEALTH CARE COVERAGE

Dear Sir:

It has come to our attention that according to our records you have failed to indicate specifically which health-care option you have chosen.

As you must realize, the grace period for such indication of said options has already passed, so consequently please be advised that if we don't hear from you *immediately*, your coverage will be determined as lapsed and subsequently terminated.

We are sure you also realize that in the event of illness, accident, or injury it is imperative to maintain continual coverage.

We look forward to your prompt reply so we might best serve you. We, of course, wish you good health and a long career.

Sincerely,

D. Base

D. Base
Health Plan Administrator

P.S. Be sure to check the mail for our new retirement package.

TEACHER TALK, CAFETERIA

Early morning:
Bad coffee brewing,
Heads nodding slowly,
Almost in time to the rhythmic bubbling.
Too sleepy to talk coherently about anything,
Let alone murder.
What else, what else, something else, please.
Last night's ball scores,
Today's toothache,
Tomorrow's retirement party.
How do you start talking about murder?
"Oh, by the way . . ."
Wanting to know the gory details,
Horrified to hear them.
Apartheid seating,
Not by color,
But by department—
Science, history, gym . . .
Apartheid by age, too.
New teachers worrying about lack of job security,
Making choices between grad school and the
    unemployment line.
Older teachers worrying about too much job security,
Making choices between early retirement and
    continuing boredom.
It's too early to talk about murder,
Isn't it?

OLIVIA TAN

I've been lucky so far—
Only been ripped off once this term, between classes,
By someone who stole my bag off my shoulder and
     ran.
In my elementary school,
Sixth graders took money from the little ones.
In my junior high,
One of my teachers was mugged.
In my first high school,
A girl was raped in the bathroom.
And now this horrible murder here in my new school.
I didn't know him well,
But should that matter?
The knots in my stomach tie and untie.
I see shadows around corners.
I hear footsteps behind me.
Sometimes, I think I'd rather be dead
Than always so afraid.
Perhaps not.
But what kind of life is it
When the only sound you hear
Is the bass drum beating of your own heart?

KEESHA TEMPLETON

Around here it's been murder,
Literally.
Vocabulary exercise of the day, guys.
How many words do we know?
Write a sentence for each.
    Period 1: manslaughter
    Period 2: homicide
    Period 3: slaying
    Period 4: assassination
    Period 5: massacre
    Period 6: ethnic cleansing
    Period 7: annihilation
    Period 8: genocide
Hey, this school is scary.
At the end of the year I'm transferrin'.
I'm just dyin' to get out.

AHMED FARRAJ

I came to United States from a small town in Yemen,
And for the first two years
They put me in classes that were too advanced for me.
The shame of my ignorance drove me away.
I learned more English from new friends
Than from my teacher, Mr. Chippendale.
I learned more from the streets
Than from his books that were too difficult.
I could not hold my anger any longer, so, soon,
I waved my discharge papers in his face,
Cursed in Arabic, and
Flung myself out of the school door
To the streets where I now drive car service.
I hear from one of my passengers
Mr. Chippendale is dead, no?
I am sorry I yelled at him and was disrespectful.
Perhaps I will return to school one day
And quietly learn my lessons.

BILL JONES—A NEIGHBORHOOD VIEW

Too many foreigners 'round here,
They should all pack up
And go back where they came from.
Then there would be more room for the rest of us—
The real Americans.
There would be less crime to worry about,
Probably one of 'em knocked off that teacher.
All they do is come over here,
Commit crimes or take away jobs,
From people who need 'em, like me.
I'm tired of having to
    Get a cab—owned by a Russian,
    Buy a newspaper—sold by an Indian,
    Hire a gypsy cab—driven by a Pakistani,
    Sample a sandwich—prepared by a Salvadorean,
    Pick up my slacks—dry-cleaned by a Korean,
    Eat a burrito—wrapped by a Mexican,
    Taste a knish—baked by an Israeli,
    Drink some beer—poured by a German,
    Take out food—fried by a Chinese,
    Wolf down a pizza—delivered by an Italian.
Stereotypes?
No, I don't know what the word means.
All I know is that there are too many foreigners
Runnin' 'round here, know what I'm sayin'?
They should all go back where they came from.

ANGELA FALCONE, GUIDANCE COUNSELOR

The air blew softly, like billowing sheets.
A summer lake somewhere, twenty years ago and
   now,
Time, present and past, caught together in slumber.
She used to be with him.
She used to love him.
And when the love was over,
It was replaced by a gentle running friendship,
Syncopated steps along a cinder track.
She saw the blue jogging suit.

"Robert, what are you doing here?"
"Looking for you, my love."
"Cut it out, you're twenty years too late."
"My fault, Ange, did you find out who did it?"
"I'm supposed to know who killed you?"
"Do this one last thing for me, hon?"
"Don't hold your breath."
"I don't have any breath to hold, remember?"
"You could always make me laugh, Robert."

She woke up,
Conscious only of an image of a summer lake
And a feeling of something she had to do.

WESLEY HARDIN

Ms. Falcone, you busy?
Can I speak to you for a minute?
The new teacher's okay, I guess,
But I sort of miss Mr. Chippendale,
Even though he caught me cheating
The day before he died.
I kinda feel bad about it.
Let's be honest, everyone cheats.
Cheating is as American as apple pie.
It's the only way to get a larger slice.
Everyone does it,
From the government on down, so
What's so bad about cheating on one little test?
Still I wish I hadn't done it.
There's no way I can
Take a makeup,
Now.

NATALIE PARKS

Ms. Falcone,
You know how the halls are between classes.
People bounce off each other
Like pinballs off bumpers,
Hitting each other with high fives,
Or, "What's up, man?"
Ms. Falcone,
You know how the rooms are during class.
People focus on the teacher,
Like deer frozen in headlights,
Writing down every word he or she says.
What I'd like to know is why
We don't talk about what matters—
Who's hurting, who's crying,
Who's losing, who's dying,
And how we are more alike
Than we are different.
I'd like to know if other people
Feel as badly as I do about Mr. Chippendale.
Or will we continue to live our lives,
Together under this roof,
Alone?

ANGELA FALCONE, GUIDANCE COUNSELOR

Natalie, what a sweet thought.
You have a class now?
See you later and we'll talk, okay?
Robert, have you become
An interchangeable cast member
In the ongoing educational sitcom?
In the halls and in the classrooms
Fragments of conversation
Rise like trial balloons and soon dissipate.
My dear Robert,
Thank you very much for your time and career,
But, you see, you've already been replaced.
That was quick, don't you think?
We've decided to sweep you and this tragedy
Under Tower High's rug.
No, no, I do not think so.

Please read the following notice:

REGARDING MR. CHIPPENDALE
Those wishing to
Express their thoughts,
Voice their grief,
Or just talk,
Are urged to see
Ms. Falcone, Room 104.

CYNTHIA ARROYO

I hate workin' here at the mall.
Is that all
At the mall?
Not according to Mr. Chippendale,
Who saw my job at Hot Dog Heaven
Not in terms of minimum wage,
But maximum opportunity.
"You want to be a writer?" he said.
"Study people's faces, not french fries.
Hear how they order, not what,
And imagine a minibiography
For each of them.
Make a connection, no matter how brief,
A short take on them while they take out.
What do you think *they* feel?
What do *you* feel about them?
Even if it's about customers and condiments.
Learning about life is a painstaking task,
But it has to be done with
Relish."

FRANK VOPUCELLI

Ms. Falcone, do you remember me?
Frank Vopucelli, Frankie.
I was lookin' for Mr. Chippendale.
Yeah, I heard.
What a cryin' shame.
He was such a good teacher,
Even though he was always on my case.
Yeah, you're right,
I did graduate last year, so
You're askin' how come I'm back from Iowa, right?
Couldn't stand lookin' at cows no more.
And I blew out my knee.
Yeah, football.
You know, it was Mr. C.
Who helped me fill out my application.
Yeah, to where the cows are.
It's not his fault things didn't work out.
Sometimes you just fumble the ball, know what I
    mean?
I'm okay now, but I have to take it easy for a while.
I could sure use his pep talk again,
Tellin' me to get off my butt
And back into the game.

HARRY BALINGER, DETECTIVE
ANGELA FALCONE, GUIDANCE COUNSELOR

"How long did you know him?"

Standard question.

"Ever since I've been here."

Standard answer.

"In what capacity?"

Were they just colleagues?

"I beg your pardon?"

What does he mean by that?

"The two of you run together?"

Several people told us that.

"Used to run."

What is he implying?

"Was he a good teacher?"

Pull back a bit.

"The best."

I miss him, miss him a lot.

"Everyone liked him, then?"

That's what I hear, too.

"Apparently not."

He's getting on my nerves.

"Any students complain about him?"

I used to hate high school.

"They complain about everybody."

Whining 101.

"Can you think of anyone specific?"

Worth a shot, why not?

"The murderer just pops up in my mind."

He's too cocky, a kid.

"Nothing rings a bell, then?"

She's hiding something.

"No."

Who am I, Quasimodo?

"Did you see him on a social basis?"	I have a gut feeling.
"Isn't that a private matter?"	*What nerve!*
"I mean no offense, my apologies."	I'll be back.
"None taken."	*Like hell.*
"Thank you for your time."	You'll be seeing me again.

SVHS - LIBRARY MEDIA CTR.

EUGENE BRAYMORE, POLICE CAPTAIN

Police work nowadays
Is a mathematical science.
Using the latest in computers,
We can graph our raw data
And determine with relative ease
Motive, suspect, and weapon.
In this case, however,
The only thing we can say right now
Is that the bullet that struck Mr. Chippendale was a
    30/30.
It came at a forty-five-degree angle,
From the roof of the high school.
There were three other shots fired as well,
Random shots, it appears.
We have patrol cars constantly cruising
A six-block-by-eight-block rectangle.
We have added more personnel,
Thereby multiplying our chances of success.
We have talked to various segments of the community,
Trying to enlarge our circle of inquiry.
No, I would not say that
We are at square one.

SVHS - LIBRARY MEDIA CTR.

LEAH TALBOT

Because of Mr. Chippendale's bothering me
(He was on me all the time),
I returned to school after a year's waitressing
To try and get my diploma.
I discovered, while away,
Life is rarely a pretty table setting
And maybe home cooking isn't too bad after all.
Some small change facts I collected along the way:
    Men get friendly too quickly.
    Skiing is great in Vermont.
    Nature is my one true friend.
    Food tastes better in the South.
    Having no money is the ultimate bummer.
    Most people are lonely.
It's not enough knowledge for one year's wandering,
But it will serve.
However, now that I'm back
And now that he's gone,
I'm getting tired of cafeteria education,
Where they throw inedible courses at you.
I'm hungry for the open road again.

EDUARDO GÓMEZ

Ms. Falcone, you know that new teacher?
The one that replaced Mr. C.?
She's short, scared, and she squirms too much.
Why doesn't she find a career that suits her?
She's timid, tense, and she talks too much.
Why would she want to teach anyway?
She's overeager and underage.
Why doesn't she just get married?
She's overdressed and underqualified.
Why doesn't she just stay home?
But, Ms. Falcone, you know somethin'?
You gotta admire her guts;
She's there every day,
Plowing through her plans,
Ignoring the noise and the yawns.
Even though she can't begin to replace Mr. C.,
Maybe she'll be okay in a couple of months—
That is, if she lasts that long.

BRIDGET LEARY

What do I remember about him?
The day I had to hand in my college application.
My essay was a mess and so was I.
Panic-stricken, I charged his desk after class.
"Please, Mr. C., you gotta read my essay—now!
Did I strike the right chord between
Truthful bragging and sincere humility?
Did I strike the right note between
Verbal virtuosity and clarity of expression?
Did I strike the right balance between
Utter coolness and passionate intensity?
Yes, all that."
"Good thing I brought my lunch," he said.
An hour later he found me, returned my essay,
Full of corrections, comments, and questions.
"Go find a typewriter, quickly," he said.
I made the deadline with minutes to spare.
Hunting and pecking, I soon came to realize
He was handing me the keys to my future.

CLAIRE D'ANGELES

Mama used to read to me from the Bible
And assured me that my place in hell
Was all but reserved.
If only I could devote my life to God,
There would be some small hope for my salvation.
But how could I demonstrate such dedication?
Me, who dreamed wicked fantasies at night.
Mr. C. heard me singing in the halls one day
And suggested I join the school chorus.
"I'm not good enough," I said shyly.
"Who says?" he asked sharply.
He personally spoke to the music department
    chairman,
Who, after an audition,
Offered me a place in his madrigal chorus.
I never got a chance to tell Mr. C.
How much I appreciated the opportunity
To show my mother that God does exist
In many houses of worship.

TOMMY SCRUGGS

For months I had looked forward to the senior trip.
I especially wanted to see Washington, D.C.
And walk through the buildings
Where history was made.
Mr. C. was one of our chaperones,
But he didn't see me drinking
In the back of the bus.
By the time we hit D.C. I was wasted
And spent two stomach-wrenching days
Sick in the bathroom of my hotel room.
On the ride back home,
Mr. C. lectured me the whole way.
Afterwards, having told me what
A complete idiot I had been,
He finally forgave me.
I hope Lincoln and Jefferson have done the same.

KIKI MARTIN

Cosmetics line the shelves;
Beauty aids line the racks;
Perfumes line the glass cases
In the quiet, pretty place where I work.
Ladies of every size and color
Softly ask me
What blush to wear,
What eyeliner to use,
What lipstick to apply.
And I tell them.
They thank me for my opinion.
School has never asked me anything,
Has never demanded anything except
Blind obedience and mindless repetition.
Mr. C. told me not to drop out,
But I said I could not survive in a world
Where garishness is the color of the day
And yelling passes for conversation.
I may go back to school one day,
But for now I'm just happy to put
A pretty face on my life.

JOHN BELLERUS

What's that sign on Falcone's door?
Grief sessions for Mr. Chippendale?
Hey, man, who ya kiddin'?
The son of a bitch failed me last term.
Teachers in this school suck,
All of 'em.
Ain't met one of 'em
That wasn't some kind of asshole.
Chippendale was the worst.
Sarcastic, man, know what I'm sayin'?
If you were gone a day, he'd say,
"How'd you do at the track?"
If you were gone a week, he'd say,
"Was Mexico nice this time of year?"
If you were gone longer than that, he'd say,
"Got tired of asking, 'Would you like fries with that,
    sir?' "
Man, I'm glad he's dead.
You wanna cut out now?
Nothin' to do here in school.
I know it's cold outside.
I got a sweatshirt

THE NOTE

Dear Ms. Falcone,

I don't know what you are doing.

I don't know what you are trying to prove.

I only know you should leave Mr. Chippendale
    alone.

Let him be forgotten, and me remembered.

He's not that important; I am.

Hey, you want to know somethin'?

There are other people I can pick off,

If I have a mind to.

It's really an arcade game,

The one where you hold a rifle

And shoot a moving mechanical bear.

If you hit him, he rears up on his hind legs

And you get points.

I don't know if the game is still around,

But my father used to take me to the carnival

When I was five or six.

I tried to shoot at the bear and missed.

I told him the rifle was kind of heavy.

"You couldn't hit the broad side of a barn," he said.

I couldn't . . .

Then.

Yes, I *was* upset in the message I left you.
Nice of you to finally return my call, Detective
    Balinger.
You're right, sarcasm isn't called for.
But listen to this note,
The one I found taped to my office door this morning.
Don't you people do your job?
You're right, criticism isn't called for.
I know you have many cases to handle.
Who are we dealing with here?
(A) a student?
(B) a psychotic?
(C) a killer?
(D) all of the above?
My life's a multiple choice test, then.
That's just great.
Look, I'm scared silly.
You're right, panic isn't called for.
Well, then, what *is* called for?
You'll pick up the note—when?
Then what?
Oh, you'll contact me when you have something?
I hope, though, the next time
I speak to you on the phone
He won't be on the line with call
Waiting.

DARREN REESE

Smooth,
Shiny,
Something I can get a good grip on.
Fast,
Furious,
Full of bang-bang action.
Elegant,
Expensive,
Exactly what I need right now.
She's some work of art.
She's always on target.
She's always by my side.
You think I'm talking about my girlfriend?
Well, think again.
I'm talking about my brand new automatic.

GEORGE PALEY, TEACHER

What's a life worth these days?
A pair of jeans?
A pair of earrings?
Maybe a car.
Or, maybe nothing at all.
He was my friend and I miss him.
We'd sit together in the English department office,
Talk about sports and summers
And how many essays English teachers have to grade.
He'd envy my family;
I'd envy his freedom.
I know that when world leaders die,
Church bells toll for them.
But what about the average person,
Like my mother, a good person, who died last year,
Like my friend, Robert, a good teacher, who died last
    month?
Who remembers?
What's a life worth these days?

LEAH TALBOT

Ms. Falcone, got a minute, maybe more?
I want to tell you something,
But I don't have the courage.
I want to get it off my chest,
But I don't have the strength.
Are people still talking about Mr. Chippendale?
Oh, just asking.
It's kind of hard to blurt this whole thing out
Without first telling you I feel like two people—
The good girl who's back in the orbit of friends and
    family,
The bad girl who's drifting far outside the pull of
    reality
You don't know why I left school in the first place, do
    you?
Mr. Chippendale did.
You might say he was the one who—
Oh, I can't do this right now.
I'll have to come back later.
I don't want to speak ill of the dead.

MIKE CURRY

Going to school is a lot like watching TV.
Click!
Channel 2: first period.
Click!
Channel 4: second period,
And so on, channel surfing throughout the day.
Watching, glassy-eyed.
The usual commercials blast at me:
Go to school,
Do your work,
Follow the rules.
Like most commercials, they're bullshit.
It's quite possible, you know,
To go through the school day
Without saying a word to any teacher.
No interactive TV here.
Subjects, like shows, change all the time.
Teachers, like fading soap stars, try to hang on.
Some, like Chippendale, are permanently cancelled.
Hey, what if they made a "Movie of the Week" about
    his murder,
Full of blood and stuff?
I'd watch it.

CLARISSA WHITFIELD

Hey, I'm okay with this place,
Really I am.
School's got breakfast and lunch.
School's got a nursery for my kid.
School's got social workers and nurses that see you for
    free.
School's got me a job workin' in the attendance office.
School's got me learnin' word processing.
School's got everythin' I want,
Except for one thing—
Safety.
School's also got knives and guns
And now murder.
Shoot, I don't want my baby growin' up
In this kind of 'vironment.
I'm always lookin' over my shoulder in the hallways.
I'm always careful talkin' to people I don't know.
I'm always carryin' some kind of razor.
How can you learn anythin' with all this violence goin'
    on?
I think I might take my chances on the streets soon.
It's probably a lot safer there.

Ms. Falcone?
A minute if you've got it.
Just stopping by to see how you're doing.
No, nothing new,
Although we're running checks on several kids
We think are carrying weapons.
They think it's a game;
We no sooner arrest them and they're out,
As quickly as you can spin a cylinder on a revolver.
Their lives are no more than violent video games.
They've got nothing to do, nothing to contribute,
     nothing to—
Sorry, I didn't mean to go on like that.
Oh, one more thing.
We obtained a warrant to go through Mr.
     Chippendale's apartment
And found a bunch of letters you had written him.
We didn't read them, exactly,
But they seemed kind of romantic.
I thought you said you just used to run track with him.
Is there more to it than that?

ANGELA FALCONE, GUIDANCE COUNSELOR

How dare you?
I want you out of my office right now.
Stop hiding behind your fake smile and polite manners
And tell me what you're getting at.
Are you charging me?
Do you think I had anything to do with his murder,
Or are you just fishing in a sea of sleaze?
His death was lurid enough.
You don't have to compound it
By putting another bullet into his memory.
I don't know what shenanigans, legal or otherwise,
You used to get those letters,
But I will not discuss them with you,
So either arrest me or
Get the hell out of my office.
You hear me?

PAIGE MCCRORY

Ms. Falcone, you ever been in love?
I'm asking you this because
I just got dumped by my boyfriend.
And I remember Mr. C. telling me, before he died,
That you were a good person to talk to.
When I told Mr. C. my secret,
That I was fifteen and my boyfriend was twenty-six,
He did not laugh,
He did not call me stupid but just said,
"Love always looks good in the morning."
I told him love looks good any time of the day.
He replied, "Paige, I was speaking metaphorically."
I didn't quite understand
Until the evening of my relationship,
When Victor dropped me for an older woman of
    nineteen,
Whom he had met at a club I wasn't allowed into.
I don't quite understand
How I could feel so great one moment
And so awful the next.
Ms. Falcone, you ever been in love?

IRINA KABANOV

In Russia, I study ballet for ten years
And see in the mirrored walls of the studio
A girl with a bright and excited face,
Eager to stretch her talent and her body.
But because life is hard in my home country
We come to America, where
To help put food on the table
I must work in my uncle's beauty salon
And see in the mirrored walls of the shop
A tired and drawn face.
I must stay on my feet,
Without dancing, for many hours.
I will save my money so I can one day
Twirl again in the mirrored world of music.
In America, there is little music but much crime.
In Russia, too, though I do not think
Teachers get shot so quickly.
In America, I must be careful where I step,
Even in school.
Just to survive, I must keep on my toes.

DARREN REESE

So you found a gun on me.
Big deal.
It wasn't loaded.
I was just holdin' it for someone.
Can't say.
You checked my locker?
You got no right to go through my shit.
What other weapons?
A box cutter,
A knife,
A bat.
No, I don't know how they got in there.
Somebody musta broken in and
Put them things in there.
How should I know?
Anybody coulda done it.
Security is so lame in this school.
No, I never used a rifle in my life.
Why you askin'?

MORTON OBERMANN, TEACHER

Teenagers are such an endangered species.
We must do our best to preserve and protect them.
Did they find a gun on that poor kid?
Aw, that's too bad.
My heart goes out to him and his family.
He must have had such a difficult life.
Obviously, he didn't know any better.
Obviously, he wasn't responsible for his actions.
I hope they treated him with respect.
I hope they read him his rights.
Did they give him a nice, comfortable cell?
Oh, how stupid of me, I forgot.
Jail is such a cruel and unusual punishment.
Of course he should be allowed to freely roam the
    streets.
A medal for self-reliance should be placed around his
    neck.
Teenagers are such an endangered species.
They must remain in their wild, natural state.
After all, it's a jungle out there.

JUNE HOGARTH

I bring my wash to the laundromat,
Drop in my quarters,
And wonder if I have the strength
To stop the vicious cycle and dry out.
My teachers thought I was just quiet and shy,
When, in reality, I was drunk and hung over.
I fooled them all,
All except Mr. C., who saw behind my glazed look
A girl tumbling and sloshing.
One day, after school, my tears overflowing,
I told him how I couldn't stop,
How my parents had thrown me out,
How I live now with my girlfriend.
And he telephoned a place where I could get help.
Still, it's a constant, day-to-day struggle
To substitute Snapple for Seagram's.
But it's possible, I think,
As my washing machine stops,
For my life to stop spinning
So I can come out clean and fresh.

ALAIN ST. MICHELLE

My parents speak to me in stop signs:
Don't hang out.
Don't come home late.
Don't mess with bad people.
And in survey questions:
Did you do your homework?
Did you study?
Did you get to school on time?
And in minisermons:
Be a role model for your little brother.
Be a credit to your parents.
Be a good citizen, above all.
America may be freer than my native Haiti,
But try telling that to my parents,
Who still treat me like a little bébé
And still practice authoritarian rule
In their own personal government-in-exile.

HERMINIO PÉREZ

As a joke, I think,
And because Mr. C. pushed it,
I applied to this prestigious Ivy League school.
As a joke, I think,
And because minority recruitment was encouraged,
I was accepted by this prestigious Ivy League school.
Well, the joke's on me
Because I'm scared shit.
I don't have the smarts;
I don't have the clothes;
I don't have any friends goin' there with me.
My girlfriend wants me to stay around her.
"You ain't leavin' me alone, are you?" she says.
My homeboys want me to stay around the
    neighborhood.
"You ain't gettin' too big in the head, are you?" they
    say.
My older sister wants me to stay around the house.
"You ain't leavin' me alone with Mama, are you?" she
    says.
In the end it was Mama from her sickbed who said,
"Estúpido, if a door is open,
It is not for the wind to rush in.
It is for the man to rush out
So the world will know he is not a joke."

MIKE CURRY

The day that teacher got shot?
It was the last exciting thing
To happen in this dumb-ass school.
Hey, most days I don't even go.
I stay home and watch TV.
I like the cartoons, man,
'Specially when they blow people away.
If I go out I go to the movies
Where you can see some really messed-up stuff.
I cheer when one hundred people die in an explosion.
I yell when a head rolls or an arm gets ripped off.
I nearly died laughing when this one time
I seen this guy get caught by a giant lawn mower
And all his body parts come flyin' out.
Maybe I'll go to Hollywood one day
And learn how they do all that stuff.
On the screen, man, big or small,
That's where reality lives.

MARVIN LEVINE

When Mr. Chippendale read *Macbeth,*
I could see the dagger floating.
When Mr. Chippendale read *Julius Caesar,*
I could hear the Senate conspiring.
When Mr. Chippendale read *Hamlet,*
I could sense the ghost walking.
The Globe Theatre of my mind
Watched Mr. Chippendale, hardly a
"Poor player that struts and frets his hour upon the
    stage,
And then is heard no more."
I remember best when he read from *The Merchant of
    Venice.*
"I am a Jew.
Hath not a Jew eyes?
Hath not a Jew hands, organs, dimensions,
Senses, affections, passions?"
Shylock asks for revenge in his world.
I ask for love in mine.
What would Shakespeare have written
If Shylock were both Jewish and gay?
Like me.

LEAH TALBOT

Ms. Falcone, you have a minute?
I don't quite know how to begin,
Except to say he should have known better.
Hell, I should have known better,
But to tell you the truth,
When I was with him
The differences in our ages
Just blurred and blended together,
Like our bodies.
And if, technically speaking,
There might have been some legal confusion
Concerning the exact age of consent,
There is no doubt that I gave my personal consent
Willingly, freely, lovingly.
I think you can guess who it is—or was.
Don't look so shocked, Ms. Falcone.
It was as much my fault as it was his.
What I did was wrong.
But what I felt was right.
I believe in my heart
That I'm being punished much too severely
Because he's in God's hands now,
And not in mine.

ANGELA FALCONE, GUIDANCE COUNSELOR

I thought I'd heard every story.
Until today.
I thought nothing could shock me.
Until now.
I thought I knew all about teenagers.
Until this moment.
Leah, have you told me the truth?
If what you've told me is true,
There is nothing I can say
That would help either one of us.
Leah, have you told me the truth?
Or is it some figment
Of a heated imagination that has confused
Love and Like,
Romance and Crush,
Passion and Pretending?
Leah, have you told me the truth?
Perhaps you've made too much of
A helpful word here,
A caring expression there?
Leah, wait, come back, don't run away.
I've got to know whether you're lying to yourself
    today
Or whether I've been lying to myself for years.

EDUARDO GÓMEZ

Ms. Falcone?
You okay?
You don't look so good.
Everything all right?
I just saw Leah run outta here.
Yeah, I know her.
I've known her since elementary school.
Jeez, that girl's nuts, always been.
The stories she makes up, unreal.
I'm related to so-and-so.
I'm going out with so-and-so.
Man, she could be on TV.
Her father's a rock star.
Her father's in the military.
Her father's a big businessman.
Yeah, right.
Her father's nowhere.
Ran out when she was ten or so.
Bummer.
You didn't know?
Just because you're a guidance counselor
Don't mean people tell you everything.
What do you mean, "Thank you"?
I didn't do nothin'.

JOHN BELLERUS

You see that new plaque for Chippendale,
The one they put up by the time clock?
What does it say: "Teacher, Scholar, Friend"?
Man, what a joke.
It should also say: "Pothead."
Yeah, you heard me right.
He caught me one time
Smokin' in a stairwell near the boys' gym.
I tried to run, but the guy tackled me,
Tackled me, would you believe.
I thought for sure he was gonna turn me over to the
     principal,
But all he did was put my bag into his pocket
And I never heard nothin' about the incident again.
Was he givin' me a chance to get straight
Or himself a chance to get baked?
Everyone thinks he was a God on high, man.
I think he was just high.

LEWIS BOARDMAN

When milk was thrown in the school cafeteria,
When kids turned over chairs in the library,
When the halls didn't feel particularly safe,
I used to play chess with Mr. Chippendale.
Not a word was spoken,
But a whole conversation took place,
Of knights and kings and castles,
Of battles lost and won at Tower High
(A most fitting name, don't you think,
For an educational institution
That is forever mired in the Middle Ages).
I still don't have a job for the summer;
I still don't know what college I'm going to.
So no doubt the techno-future will pass me by
As I prefer medieval meditation
Over a chessboard where I now play both sides.
I'll take my time, thank you,
To sit here and plot my next move,
Without him.

P. J. COMPSON

The book you gave me is way too long.
The print is too small
And I don't understand some of the longer words.
The story is boring.
I don't care if she refuses his love for two hundred
     pages.
If he's so horny let him find someone else.
I don't care if she has to wear an *A* on her chest.
Everyone fools around these days.
I don't care if the daughter is illegitimate.
Nobody cares about that anymore.
Reading is like swimming through molasses, man.
Where's the rape? The murder? The action?
I gotta go, man.
The teacher's showing a video in my next class.

VANESSA RHODES

When Mr. Chippendale said
I should apply to a college out of my league,
I thought he was crazy for suggesting it.
"Give it a shot," he said. "You never know."
"Yeah, right, they're going to accept me," I said,
    months ago.
"Yeah, right, they did accept me," I said, last week.
However, there is one problem:
Both my parents work.
I'm sorry about that.
We have two cars.
I'm upset about that.
Our private home is nearly all paid up.
I'm agitated about that.
Because, educationally speaking,
Poorer is better.
According to university formulas,
My family has too much money
To qualify for financial aid
And not enough to send me without it.
I'm almost glad I don't have to tell Mr. C.
That I'm too rich to afford
The college of my choice.

DOMINICK MARTELLI, NEIGHBORHOOD BUSINESSMAN

I dropped outta school when I was fifteen.
My father, not pleased at all, said,
"Now you will see what work really is."
And so I did, sweating six days a week
In my father's butcher shop.
I learned there were no shortcuts to
Carving out a life for myself.
I see the kids from the local high school walk by,
Even hire a few now and then to help out.
They can't spell or subtract or sweep.
If they work for more than ten minutes,
They think it's overtime.
I wonder what they learn in that school.
I wonder who can teach them,
Who would want to teach them.
Looking back, I was lucky.
I had the best instructor.
My father was a cut above most people I've met.
I'm proud to say I'm a chip off the old
Butcher's block.

KARYN MILLER

The nights are bad,
When giant heads, like basketballs,
Bounce past me
And giant mouths, like open wounds,
Scream in my ear.
I keep seeing Mr. C.'s head, lifting, falling,
Again and again,
A never-ending video loop
Projected in front of my eyes.
The days are better,
When the soft shuffle of my slippers,
Along with my medication,
Blunt the hard-core edges
Of that violent video clip.
I can't wait until the tape
Stops rewinding,
Then replaying,
And is ejected from my memory for good.

ROSINA ROBLES

In my home country,
When the teacher walks into the room,
We all stand up and say, "Good morning, sir."
In this country,
When the teacher walks into the room,
We all turn in our seats and continue talking.
In my home country,
Whole villages would collect school fees
For the brightest boys.
Because I was neither the brightest nor a boy,
Mama and I left our home country
To look for a good job for her
And a good school for me.
Do not American students realize how lucky they are?
In my home country only the rich—usually boys—
Get into the finest schools.
In this country learning costs little for boys *and* girls.
You can do or become whatever you want.
Just because education is free in this country,
Does not mean it is worth
Less.

My grandfather does not tell me his war stories.
He will, to a point, but then declares the good parts
Classified material.
Sometimes, when he is in the mood,
He will begin to tell me about
The preparation for the invasion,
The English countryside, the Scottish girls.
He tells me about
Climbing down cargo nets,
Jumping into landing craft,
And wading into the water
(Which changed color, he said).
Then he abruptly stops as if cut down
By a sniper's bullet.
I want to hear the gory parts.
I tell him about the teacher who got shot in school,
As if that would put us on even killing fields.
"It's not the same thing," he says,
Getting this faraway look in his eyes
As he drifts over time, continents, and water.
Those who know history
Are condemned to relive it, I think.
My grandfather does not tell me his war stories.

THE RED-HOODED SWEATSHIRT

Cool stories in the papers lately:
Mother and daughter step into a crosswalk,
Get splattered by a truck.
Girl goes to her high school prom,
Gets wiped out by a falling piece of concrete.
Man buys his paper at the local newsstand,
Gets blown away by a guy robbing the owner.
All proof you gotta avoid
The wrong places at the wrong time.
I avoid all the wrong places,
Like home, school, and work.
I go to the park instead,
Where I sit watching the pigeons fight for crumbs.
Then I walk right up to them,
Through their tight circle.
They scatter;
I pull out my pellet gun
And see how many I can shoot.
It's a matter of luck which ones live.

HARRY BALINGER, DETECTIVE

Just checking to see if you're okay, Ms. Falcone.
You're not still angry with me, are you?
Just doing my job,
Which I don't mind telling you
Is a lot rougher these days.
Kids sure were different when I was in high school.
They'd beat each other up then, no weapons, like now.
I remember a police lineup we had around last
    Christmas,
Of fourteen-year-olds.
Each boy looked so angelic—
And yet one of the boys,
Who was identified by a kid wrapped in bandages,
Had sliced and diced a face so horribly
That the emergency-room doctor told me
There were strips of flesh just hanging.
I tell you this because no one is innocent.
Everyone has a mental safe-deposit box
Full of dark secrets and regrets.
Take your Mr. Chippendale, for example.
We found his name in a notebook
On the body of a numbers collector
We discovered in a ditch last night.
Tell me, Ms. Falcone, if Mr. Chippendale had a
    gambling problem.
Please don't get angry with me again.
I'm just trying to track down all leads.

JOHN BELLERUS

Oh, man, what a shit day.
The way I feel right now,
If I had a gun in my pocket,
I'd shoot somebody,
I swear I would.
I'd shoot
The cop who gave me
My second parking ticket in a week;
My counselor, Ms. Falcone,
Who said I'll have to go to summer school;
My old girlfriend, who thinks
The louder she screams,
The more I'll listen.
I'd quit school right now and get a job,
If there were any jobs to get.
I remember that creep Chippendale saying
That the whole world is waiting for us.
Yeah, right.
Waiting for us to fall flat on our asses.
Why do they keep lyin' to us, man?
I don't understand it.
What a shit life.

PAIGE MCCRORY

Oh, man, what a great day.
The way I feel right now,
If I had some money in my pocket,
I'd give it away,
I swear I would.
I'd give it to
The cop who let me go,
Even though I ran a stop sign;
My counselor, Ms. Falcone,
Who said I have enough credits to graduate early;
My new boyfriend, who thinks
That whatever I do is wonderful,
Even if it isn't.
I can't wait to finish school and go to college,
There being so many colleges to choose from.
I remember that wonderful Mr. Chippendale saying
That the whole world is waiting for us.
That's right.
Waiting for us to stand up tall.
Why do they keep doing so much for us?
I don't understand it.
Oh, man, what a great life.

KEESHA TEMPLETON

Too much waitin' around in this world.
Too many of my male friends
Waitin' for somethin' to wake 'em up.
Too many of my female friends
Waitin' for their little ones to fall asleep.
Too much waitin' around in class,
Learnin' nothin'.
Too much waitin' in the halls,
Watchin' nothin'.
Me, I got big plans.
I'm gonna graduate,
Get my own job,
Get my own place,
Far from here where there's no
Waitin' around for any man
Or any check.
Here, you want my business card?
You better get in touch with me quick.
I ain't waitin' around
For nothin'.

LEWIS BOARDMAN

My father always promised me he'd live forever.
Unfortunately, he didn't live up to his promise.
All I have left now are
Snapshots of memories in my mind:
A trip through his office building,
A ride on the roller coaster,
A drive through the countryside.
My father took me everywhere.
In school, Mr. C. became my surrogate father,
Books providing new parameters:
A trip through ancient Greece,
A ride on Route 66,
A drive through the streets of London.
But when Mr. C. died,
I did not want to go anywhere.
I stopped reading altogether
And sat in my room,
Motionless.

ENID POPKIN

I used to think of setting up
Mr. Chippendale with my mother,
Their both being single and all.
It would have been cool
Having a teacher for a stepdad.
Ms. Falcone, you wanna go to a wedding?
Yeah, you're right, my mom doesn't waste any time.
Yep, number four, that's it.
The last one, number three, my step-stepfather,
Took off when I was thirteen.
He's somewhere out west—Utah, I think.
Yeah, he writes, but postcards aren't enough.
Hey, so now my mother's planning to get married
    again,
Says it's for real this time.
I have my doubts.
Ms. Falcone, you can come as my guest, if you want.
Don't worry if you miss it, though.
You can always catch the next one.

ANGELA FALCONE, GUIDANCE COUNSELOR

Wedding?
That's nice of you to invite me, Enid,
But I don't feel much like celebrating these days.

What's wrong with me?
I sit around solving the world's problems
And do not work on my own:
Why I watch too much TV,
Why I read too many trashy novels,
Why I eat way too much,
Why I keep thinking of the past—
When I wrote poetry,
When I traveled to Italy,
When I met Robert,
When my life had a lightness to it.
Robert, I try not to listen to all the negatives,
But what is the truth about you, me, us?
Black holes appear in the constellation of my
    memories.
I still have to know who you were, why you died,
And why I can't let you go.

ANOTHER NOTE

Ms. Falcone,
Forget about my other note.
I didn't mean to scare you.
I didn't mean to harm you.
You ain't done nothin' to me.
I only want to explain 'bout
Pigeons, rifles, and Mr. C.
But if I came in to tell you my story,
Would you listen to me,
Or run screamin' to the police?
Maybe I want
My name in the news,
My friends knowin' who I am,
My interview with Geraldo.
But maybe I don't need
The police lockin' me up,
The judge throwin' away the key,
The warden pullin' the switch.
Look, I gotta have the glory.
Ain't you seen <u>Natural Born Killers</u> on video?
I need the bright lights of fame.
Only I don't want 'em to burn me
Beyond recognition.

HARRY BALINGER, DETECTIVE

Ms. Falcone?
I want to bring you up to speed
Regarding our investigation.
That is, if you'll still allow me into your office.
That's right, I'm just doing my job.
No, we haven't come up with anything definite yet,
But the second note you gave us is quite promising.
It was typed on a computer,
Perhaps one here at school.
A student?—That's a distinct possibility.
We feel that the individual involved is torn
Between giving and not giving himself up—
Right—herself up is also conceivable.
He or she may even walk into your office,
Just to taunt you or talk to you.
What do you mean, "speed up the process"?
What kind of idea?
What assembly program?
What fifteen minutes?
You want to tell me what you have in mind?
I don't know what you mean by
"Drawing the killer out into the bright lights."

BRETT OGILVIE

Had I crossed the intersection
Five seconds sooner or later,
The drunken driver wouldn't have hit me.
Had I argued with my mother
Five seconds more or less,
The drunken driver wouldn't have demolished my car.
Had I even found my comb
Five seconds earlier or later,
The drunken driver would have zoomed right past me.
I'm thinking of these accidents of time
As I lie in my hospital bed for the third month.
The doctors say I'm lucky to be alive.
I don't quite see it that way.
Then I think of Mr. Chippendale
(The only teacher to visit me here),
And wonder if he would be alive today
Had he run five seconds faster or slower.
I guess I'm the lucky one after all,
Because I'm the one who has
Countless seconds, minutes
Hours, years, before me.

LEAH TALBOT

I knew the moment it was over.
You, saying, "It has gotten out of hand,"
While still in my arms.
Me, listening to the whispers behind my back,
Instead of your whispers in my ear.
Was it a dream that I loved you?
Perhaps, but isn't love a dream that floats
Above the ordinary Muzak of the day?
Isn't it the bright circus calliope of joy,
Not the daily marching band rhythm of class after
    class?
I only felt alive when I was with you,
And when I wasn't with you,
I squirreled away the memory chestnuts of our time
    together.
But I got greedy; I wanted more of you than
    memories.
I wanted time—free, open, shout-it-from-the-hilltops
    time.
You backed away; I ran away, only to realize
How much I missed you.
When I came back, I could tell from your eyes, Robert,
You had made a choice between literature and life,
Prose and passion—and it wasn't me, love.
Better judgment prevailed, no doubt,
Better judgment flattening forever
The grace note of my life.

WESLEY HARDIN

They say they are
Looking for a few good men.
I think I'm one of them.
I know who Montezuma was
And where Tripoli is.
I am ready to fight for my country
On the land or on the sea.
I can do push-ups and run wind sprints.
I can take a rifle apart
And put it back together.
I'm an expert shot (my father showed me),
And I know I'd look great in dress blues.
The only difficult thing was the armed-forces test.
I was tempted to cheat,
But I had been through that with Mr. C.
To be one of the few and the proud
You gotta start by being honest
To the core.

JOHN BELLERUS

You want to suspend me?
Just because of a little fight?
That's messed up, man.
It wasn't my fault.
He bumped into me.
He didn't say he was sorry,
Showed me no respect.
He called me names; he called my mother names.
I ain't havin' that.
So his nose got busted.
Serves him right for puttin' it in my business.
Am I sorry for what I did?—Hell, no!
I'm never sorry for what I do, man.
Whaddya mean, did I have a fight
With any teacher recently?
I'd knock over anyone who starts with me.
You ain't suspendin'
The guy with the busted nose?
Where's the justice in that, man?

BARNEY, THE NEIGHBORHOOD DEALER

I, Barney, the neighborhood dealer
Am finding it tough these days.
Nobody is buyin' from me anymore.
The young punks are growin' their own,
The older guys want better merchandise.
Even the cops have better things to do than hassle me.
My old raincoat (with its many secret pockets)
Fell apart in a sudden storm.
You should pardon the expression,
But I feel naked without it.
My shoes and hat were stolen by junkies.
My social worker keeps pestering me about therapy.
My priest wants me to fill out job-training applications.
After wiring my sister in Tulsa for money
I purchased a new raincoat,
A London Fog with a special zipper front
(And many more pockets).
The young punks hit on me for change.
The older guys praise my good taste in outerwear.
The cops tell me to get rid of the coat
On account of the sunny weather.
I, Barney, the neighborhood dealer,
Am finding it tough these days.

JAMES HARRINGTON

I told you everything;
I don't know who he was,
Some old guy in a raincoat.
Like I said,
The light turned green in my favor,
And he just walked out,
Right in front of me.
How should I know if he was trying to kill himself?
Hey, look, I'm late for work.
How much longer is this going to take?
How many more questions do I have to answer?
Look, I'm in a rush.
No, I don't know who he was, told you that.
What do I care?

VERA JACOB, TEACHER

We shared the same birthday
And usually the same lunch period—
Cafeteria friends for a few years.
I thought we were going to share
The same life spans as well.
After your funeral, Robert,
I suffered a mild heart attack.
Recuperating at home, I asked myself
What I would want written on my tombstone.
The word that came back to me was:
TEACHER.
I've been at Tower for over fifteen years
And with your death, Robert,
I have begun to feel the chill of my own mortality.
I'll go back to teaching soon, I'm sure.
It's the only thing I know how to do well.
But I'll miss you sitting across from me
At our usual table in the cafeteria.
Oh, how you made me laugh.

AGNES RINSKA

In Poland, I felt I was living in perpetual winter
On the desolate, windswept landscape of my soul,
Which froze my heart to every person I was close to.
I lashed out at family and friends to exorcise
The darkness I felt inside of me.
And so when Josef, a much older family friend
(Who always desired me, I could tell)
Returned from America where he has a business,
I asked him to marry me and take me to the U.S.
It was an economic marriage, not a romantic one,
And when he came to realize that I wanted
My own bed, not his, I was ready with my own green
    card.
I lied about my age, for I look very young and
    beautiful,
And enrolled in this high school to learn English more.
I do not speak to Josef anymore,
Nor do I communicate with my parents.
I have driven everyone away.
In college I want to study criminology.
I want to study patterns of deviant behavior
And wish to understand more
My own crimes against humanity.

YING LI

In China, I saw some American TV,
Western movies and "I Love Lucy."
This is what America is like, I thought.
When my family came to this country,
I was placed in Mr. Chippendale's beginning English
   class.
Every day, beautiful new words
Would come to me like small presents.
I felt proud when he praised me
And when he died I was very much sorry.
The new teacher was not so nice and didn't praise me.
I learned my English from TV.
I learned words that would horrify my mother.
I learned talk-show guests tell horrible things.
I learned rest of the world does not exist.
And I learned violence and sex on TV
Kill all the beautiful words.
This is what America is like, I think,
All speed and violence and
No beautiful words.

DARREN REESE

Last summer, I went with my uncle
North of the neighborhood, about two hundred miles,
To a small town, with no traffic lights,
To watch the July Fourth pageant.
It seemed like a foreign country.
There were bands.
There were fire engines.
There were floats pulled by pickup trucks.
There were patriotic songs.
And when it grew dark, there were fireworks.
A thousand men, women, and children
Sat on a hillside, their white faces
Reflected in the red, white, and blue of exploding
    shells.
They looked at me as if I were an alien.
They looked at me as if to say
"What are you doin' here?"
This summer, I'm stayin' in my own neighborhood,
With my own crew,
So I don't have to see reflected
"In the rockets' red glare"
Faces that sing about freedom and brotherhood,
But don't know nothin' about it.

CLAIRE D'ANGELES

To honor Mr. Chippendale,
Ms. Falcone has asked me
To write a song for a memorial program.
Of course, I said yes
For the man who opened up the musical door for me.
I tell my mother, who wants me
To come home straight away,
I must stay late in school
To compose my piece, note by note.
"Why can you not do this in class?" she asks.
"There's no time to do anything creative in class," I
    reply.
With five-minute breaks between classes,
Ten-minute quizzes,
Thirty-minute tests,
Forty-five-minute periods,
There is scarcely enough time to breathe.
I wish for my song to be perfect,
For it to rise slowly and directly to heaven.
Mr. Chippendale could then take his sweet time
In listening to my solo,
Measure for measure.

CELIA CAMPBELL

To honor Mr. Chippendale,
Ms. Falcone has asked me
To write a poem for the memorial program.
Of course, I said yes
For the man who opened up the literary door for me.
There isn't a country I haven't visited,
A person I haven't met,
A crisis I haven't encountered
Whenever I wrap myself, cocoonlike,
In the comforting blanket of a book.
My mother yells, "Get a friend."
My father yells, "Get a job."
My sister yells, "Get a life."
Little do they know I have all three
Whenever I float myself, fetuslike,
In the comforting womb of a book.
I may never be able
To expel myself from this neighborhood,
But I thank Mr. C. for my literary delivery.
I will thank him with the best poem I can write.

MARVIN LEVINE

Quick!
What do you remember best about high school?
It's all in the yearbook:
The first day of classes,
The best teacher you had,
The winning basketball season.
Quick!
What are you trying to forget about high school?
It's not in the yearbook:
The first day of classes,
The worst teacher you had,
The losing football season.
My best memory?
Easy.
English class with Mr. Chippendale,
Particularly the day he said to me
In front of the whole class,
"Mr. Levine, that is a positively brilliant insight,"
When I said the true hero of *Billy Budd* was Captain
    Vere.
No other day in four years ever came close.
Of course, Ms. Falcone, I'll say a few words
To honor him at the memorial.

ANNAMARIE PARISI

School Cafeteria—
Lunchtime Map of the World:

The Russian Tables	The Korean Tables
The Hispanic Tables	The Arab Tables
The Chinese Tables	The African-American Tables
The Greek Tables	The Irish Tables
The Indian Tables	The Pakistani Tables

And me, at the Italian Tables, of course,
Continents separated by condiments,
Not oceans.
Integration, a phrase for the civics book,
Not the salad bar.
Friendship, a euphemism for politeness,
Not for togetherness.
Today I went across the border
To ask Mustapha for his math homework
And got such a look from the girls at my table.
Maybe I'll just split and grab some takeout.
Then it won't matter where I sit or stand.
Tomorrow, instead of lunch,
We are all going to assembly to honor Mr. C.,
From different sections of the auditorium, of course.

HARRY BALINGER, DETECTIVE

Ms. Falcone, I want to go over
Our arrangements for the assembly tomorrow.
We will have many plainclothes officers
Stationed at strategic points around the building.
"Better to be safe than sorry"—
That's what my father always used to say.
He and I used to fight a lot when I was in high school.
He worked for the highway department,
Constructing roads that ran in parallel lines,
Much like his life and mine.
He thought I didn't have the sense to know
Whether to go through or around obstacles,
Much like the roads he built.
But when I graduated from the academy,
He said I had chosen the right path after all.
Yet with this investigation, I must tell you
I find myself on a road leading nowhere,
Which is why I'm willing to follow your hunch.
Your memorial program might be just the way to go,
The route to lead the murderer, without detours,
Right back to us, his license to kill revoked.

ANGELA FALCONE, GUIDANCE COUNSELOR

Three o'clock in the morning
And I can't sleep.
You would think that by this time, Robert,
You'd have the good graces
Not to invade my dreams anymore.
It's probably the memorial,
The many details I must attend to,
The songs, the poems, the tributes,
So it all goes smoothly tomorrow,
More smoothly than my troubled tossing.
I never got the chance at the funeral
To metaphorically close the coffin.
I never got the chance to ask
Whether you were in pain, or past it.
Most important of all,
I never got the chance to tell you
That I have always loved you,
And the memory of my love,
Keeps me awake and alive, even now—
Especially now.
May you rest in peace, Robert,
Even if I can't.

RUSSELL FRANKS, PRINCIPAL

I would like to thank the following people
For putting together this splendid memorial
I'd like to thank
Claire D'Angeles for her song,
Celia Campbell for her poem,
And Marvin Levine for his words.
I'd especially like to thank our own Ms. Falcone
For her professional expertise and tireless devotion
In bringing this whole enterprise together.
The orchestra, the chorus—all simply splendid.
Mr. Chippendale enjoyed the respect of his peers
And the admiration of his students.
Let us not forget him.
Now remember, when you hear the bell,
Walk quickly and quietly to your next class.

"Why'd we have to go to this assembly?"
"Dunno. Homeroom teacher made us."
"What's the big deal? The guy was only a teacher."
"Yeah, I know. You wanna cut out? I'm bored."
"Cool."
"Hey, what's the dead guy's name again?"
"I forgot."

ANGELA FALCONE, GUIDANCE COUNSELOR

Pardon me, Principal Franks,
If I might say a final word
To the students before the bell rings?
Yes, I'll be brief.

Ladies and gentlemen,
There are many people who say man is basically evil,
That the evil is part of his nature,
That he cannot live without bringing pain and death.
When I look into your faces,
I reject that belief.
When I look into your faces,
I see kindness, humor, and hope.
I see a world where good men are memorialized
And felons are forgotten.
Mr. Chippendale's character will be remembered.
His killer's cowardice won't,
Not even for fifteen minutes.
This killer will remain
Anonymous, amorphous, attention-less.
No one will know his name.
No one will know his story.
No one will notice him at all.
I, Angela Falcone, guarantee that.
Good-bye, Mr. Chippendale,
We will always love and remember you

LEAH TALBOT

My father left when I was ten,
A departure of his own choosing.
And when I realized he was not coming back
I swore that I would never open up to any man again.
I took what I could from men—good times, better
    presents—
Before, inevitably, they would hit the road as well.
In the night, week, or month of a relationship,
I learned about the low cost of leaving,
A departure of my own choosing.
But when I grew to love you,
I was torn between my wanting to stay,
And your wanting to go.
It was a lovely memorial, Robert.
You would have gotten a big kick out of it, I'm sure.
You men are all alike, though.
You come—
And then go.
I suppose I now have to accept that
The ending of our relationship was
A departure of your own choosing.
But Robert, I'd still like to know,
Why did you have to abandon me,
Too,
Twice?

MIKE CURRY

Ms. Falcone? Can I come into your office?

That was some cool program you ran last period

I liked it; it made him sound like a famous person,

A movie star or somethin' like that.

I think you're wrong, though, about murderers being
   forgotten.

Plenty of bad guys get remembered.

I wanna be famous, too, one day.

Maybe like in the movies, one of those guys

Who get to climb the outside of buildings,

Or get to shoot hundreds of people,

Like this movie I seen where

This German World War II guy

Is standing on a balcony with this big rifle,

And he's just pickin' off people, left and right,

Like it's no big deal. So cool.

People were fallin' down all over the place. Hysterical,
   man.

Why are you lookin' at me like that, funny like?

Anyway, I gotta get to class.

You seen my red sweatshirt?

I swear I had it when I came in here.

Okay, okay, I'll wait.

Who do you want me to meet?

Mr. Balinger?

Is he a new teacher?

Is he gonna replace Mr. Chippendale?

EPILOGUE:

ROLL CALL

(Thirteen Years Later)

Ms. Angela Falcone	retired, traveling somewhere in Europe
Principal Russell Franks	dead of a coronary three years ago
Mike Curry	tried as an adult, convicted, served five years, moved to Alaska to hunt, fish, and make movies
Detective Balinger	now Captain Balinger of the sixteenth precinct
John Bellerus	corrections officer
Darren Reese	insurance salesman, new homeowner
Kiki Martin	ex–runway model, fashion consultant
Celia Campbell	university professor, poet
Enid Popkin	bridal shop owner
Leah Talbot	hostess, four-star restaurant
Lewis Boardman	history teacher, Tower High School
Annamarie Parisi	social worker
Karyn Miller	director, day care center, married, four children

In the early morning light,
Roberta Chartoff, a new English teacher,

Walks up the front steps of the school,
Eager to step onto the educational wonderwheel.
Cautiously, she approaches the main office
And notices a little plaque to the left of the time clock.
It reads:

ROBERT CHIPPENDALE
TEACHER, SCHOLAR, FRIEND

"Who's that?" she wonders,
As she punches in at 7:04.

ABOUT THE AUTHOR

Mel Glenn was born in Switzerland, grew up in Brooklyn, New York, and was a Peace Corps volunteer in Sierra Leone, West Africa. He has been teaching English for twenty-six years at his alma mater, Lincoln High School, in Brooklyn. He and his wife, Elyse, live in Brooklyn with their two children, Jonathan and Andrew.

He is the author of four award-winning books of poetry and three novels. Among his poetry books, *Class Dismissed* was an ALA Best Book for Young Adults, an ALA Best Book of the Best Books, and a Society of Children's Book Writers Golden Kite Honor Book. *Class Dismissed II* won the Christopher Award and was a *School Library Journal* Best Book of the Year, and *My Friend's Got This Problem, Mr. Candler* was an ALA Best Book for Young Adults.